Lost in the Hills

Julia Golding ■ Mark Beech,
Yannick Robert,
James Cottell and Emi Ordas

Contents

OXFORD
UNIVERSITY PRESS

The Lost Office

By Julia Golding

Illustrated by Mark Beech

Sophie and her grandmother stepped on to the platform and watched the train pull away.

Gran counted the shopping bags. "Holiday clothes, sandals, sun hat, library books … What have I forgotten?" she said.

"Your umbrella!" cried Sophie.

They looked at each other in dismay. Granddad had given Gran the duck-headed umbrella a long time ago. She said it was like always having him with her.

"When did you last have it?" asked Sophie. Gran took out a handkerchief and dabbed her eyes. "Not since we got on the train this morning. It has been such a busy day, I forgot all about it." She patted her heart. "Oh, how I wish I had paid attention!"

"Gran, why don't you sit in the café while I see if it has been handed in?"

"Would you? You do look after me."

Leaving Gran with a pot of tea to soothe her, Sophie left to search the station.

After a while, down a narrow alley, Sophie saw a tiny sign saying 'Lost Office'.

It's so tucked away I'm surprised anyone finds this place, she thought.

The windows of the office were too grimy to see inside. The black door had a knocker in the shape of a question mark. Sophie reached up but before she could knock the door creaked open.

"Hello?" called Sophie.

Inside, it was very dark. A man crouched over a thick book, writing with a crimson quill. Boxes towered over him and the only light came from a lamp by his elbow.

"Excuse me?" said Sophie.

"Yes? What have you lost?" snapped the man. He looked frail, like a paper doll dressed in a black suit. A brass nameplate in front of him said 'Mr Ree'.

"An umbrella. Shall I describe it to you?"

Mr Ree carried on scribbling. "No. Find it yourself. Umbrellas that way." He pointed down the corridor behind him.

"Um, thanks," mumbled Sophie.

Sophie knew she couldn't be too long or Gran would worry. She hurried past Mr Ree.

People lost so many amazing things. In one aisle she passed a mountain of magazines, a heap of handbags, a basket of phones, including early mobiles the size of bricks, and a flag parade of scarves, which rustled gently as she moved past.

No time for exploring, though. She had to find the umbrella. Looking around, she could no longer see the exit. The corridor had vanished behind a rail of coats, or was it behind the books, or maybe behind the rows of birdcages? The cages were mostly empty but one had a nest inside. The songbird sitting on its eggs trilled angrily at her so she edged back. Birds fluttered overhead.

"Hello? Mr Ree? Er, I seem to be lost. Can you direct me to the umbrellas, please?" Sophie half-shouted. She was starting to get worried.

No reply. *Mr Ree really shouldn't let customers go wandering off with no idea how to find what they are looking for*, thought Sophie.

She pulled out her phone. No signal.

Don't panic. I'll just have to escape unaided, Sophie thought. *That green cape looks familiar*. She headed towards it.

The cape hid the door to a room full of picnic baskets. They were all empty, only a few crumbs left at the bottom of each. A couple of birds pecked at these hungrily. She backed out quickly – and bumped into someone.

Sophie yelped.

"Apologies! I didn't mean to startle you," said a boy standing behind her. He was dressed in a long jacket and PE shorts. A tie was wrapped round his head to keep back his straggly hair. He was very pale, as if he hadn't been outside for months. His eyes were kind, though, and full of curiosity.

"Who are you?" they asked together.

The boy laughed. "I'll go first. Logan Hart, at your service." He gave her a bow. "Forgive my attire – I have to use what I can find."

"Hi, Logan. I'm Sophie. I'm lost. You too?"

"Yes, of course. We are all lost in the Lost Office," Logan answered.

A dog bounded out of the shadows and bumped into Sophie's legs. It was a labrador, with brown eyes. He sniffed her pockets hopefully.

"That's Digby. He got left as a puppy. He's been a good companion for me," said Logan.

As Digby was now a full-grown dog, Sophie began to realize how long Logan had been lost for.

"Do you mean you've been here over a *year*?" asked Sophie.

Logan shrugged. "Feels like forever. Once you're lost, you're lost for good in the Lost Office. Unless you find the object you are seeking."

"What? Haven't you found yours?" Sophie's alarm grew.

Logan scratched Digby's neck. "I came looking for my sandwiches but I think the birds got to them first. Something about this place seems to make things stay lost forever. It's a mystery but I think Mr Ree is at the bottom of it."

Sophie shivered. "I'm stuck here unless I find the umbrella?"

"Correct. It isn't that simple, though. You won't find it by looking for it."

"So how *will* I find it?"

"You're not *supposed* to find it." Logan sighed. "I would give anything to get out of here. I don't even know what half the stuff is that gets left here these days."

"When did you arrive?" asked Sophie.

Logan showed her the back of the door to the picnic room. He had scratched out a calendar.

"Time seems to get lost in this place, too." He sighed.

Sophie couldn't bear the idea of staying there for even a day, let alone a century. Not even with two new friends. She had to get back to Gran. She had an idea.

"You say, if I look I won't find it?" Sophie asked.

"That's right," said Logan.

"What if you and Digby look?" asked Sophie hopefully.

Logan's face broke into a delighted smile. "By George, I think you might be on to something! What did you say you'd lost?"

Sophie described the umbrella.

"There are so many umbrella rooms here. Does it have a particular smell? Digby is very good at sniffing things out, aren't you, Digby?" said Logan.

"Roses. Gran's favourite soap."

"Digby, you know what to do," said Logan.

The dog wagged his tail, sniffed and shot off down a narrow aisle. He led them into a room filled with umbrellas, stacked tightly together on the shelves so only the handles showed.

"I see it!" cried Sophie, pointing towards the top of the shelf. The duck's beak poked out.

Nooo!!

Logan tugged her back. "Don't move! If you try to get the umbrella, it will vanish and go somewhere else. Let me." He pulled out some handles to make a ladder. He climbed and grabbed the duck.

"Catch!" he shouted, throwing the duck-headed handle towards Sophie.

As her hand closed round the umbrella, a shriek echoed through the labyrinth. "Nooo!"

Mr Ree came running in, wringing his hands. "All my lovely lost things!" he wailed.

Objects flew off the walls and whirled around, then disappeared out of windows, down corridors and even up the chimney. "You've ruined it!" Mr Ree cried.

"No, we've found it," said Sophie, waving Gran's umbrella at him.

The lost property cleared and a door opened behind Logan. A horse-drawn carriage rumbled by outside and a steam train chugged over a viaduct.

"Good. Not much has changed while I've been away. Thank you, Miss Sophie." Logan whistled to Digby. "Come along, boy. There's a basket by the fire for you at home."

A second door on the opposite side of the room creaked open. Train announcements echoed in the distance.

"Thank you!" Sophie bowed to Logan.

Logan laughed and darted into the sunshine, Digby at his heels.

Before Mr Ree could stop her, Sophie ran through her door. Looking up at the sign over the door, Sophie saw the words had changed to: Found Office.

The windows were now bright and the lady behind the desk looked friendly.

Sophie ran back to the café. She arrived just as Gran was finishing her tea.

"Oh, thank you, darling." Gran hugged the umbrella, eyes shining. "I hope it wasn't too much trouble?"

"It was a bit of an adventure but I found it in the end – with some help," said Sophie.

Far away, a dog barked and a newly hatched brood of songbirds flew the nest.

Walking into Danger

By Julia Golding

Illustrated by Yannick Robert

Luke, Skyler and Connor are on a school trip in the hills.
Mist descends and the three of them become separated from
the rest of their class.

Message in a Bottle

By Julia Golding

Illustrated by James Cottell

Setting the scene

 DYLAN loves exploring. He is independent and a natural leader.

 SAMIRA often gets bored and would rather eat ice cream than explore the seaside!

 CARLOS is happy to do most things!

 GRANDDAD is in his late 70s and was a boy during World War II. Dylan is his grandson. He is happy for the children to play at the seaside, remembering what it was like when he was a child.

The setting: The three friends are on holiday by the sea with their families. We open the play in the morning outside Dylan's holiday cottage. Dylan suggests they explore a little rocky cove which his granddad used to go to as a child.

The children are sitting outside DYLAN'S holiday house, which is near the beach.

DYLAN: What do you want to do this morning?

SAMIRA: Nothing can beat yesterday's bodyboarding.

CARLOS: My dad says it's too rough for that today. We have to stay on the beach.

DYLAN: I know. Let's explore! Granddad told me about a little cove just round the headland with great rock pools. He used to go there all the time when he was a child. He hasn't been there since the war. He said it was always too dangerous.

CARLOS: Is it safe now?

DYLAN: Yes, but you can only walk there at low tide *(checks watch)* and that's now. *(leading the others into the house)* Granddad, is it OK if we go to the cove?

GRANDDAD: Fine by me. Take your phone with you. Watch the tide and don't get too close to the cliffs. *(waving)* I only wish I could come with you!

SAMIRA:	(grumbling and dragging her feet) Do we have to explore? Can't we just buy an ice cream?
DYLAN:	Stay here if you want to but we're going, aren't we, Carlos? (starts running and Carlos follows)
SAMIRA:	(catching up) Not fair!

The children run down the beach. CARLOS and SAMIRA run into the sea. DYLAN stays on the sand.

SAMIRA:	It's so cold!
DYLAN:	No, not in the sea! Come on, you two. (starting to walk off)
SAMIRA:	(now laughing and splashing Carlos) Hey, where's Dylan going?

CARLOS: To his granddad's cove, remember! He's a man on a mission!

SAMIRA: Race you there!

DYLAN rounds the headland first and reaches a hidden inlet.

DYLAN: Hey, guys, I think this is it!

CARLOS and SAMIRA join him.

CARLOS: Wow! I see what your granddad means. It's like a secret world.

DYLAN: Neptune's hideout. This rock is his throne. *(sits)* Behold me, sea creatures, your king! *(CARLOS throws seaweed at him.)* OK, perhaps not.

SAMIRA: *(stepping into the pool)* This rock pool's so deep – and warm! Argh – a crab! *(clambering out quickly)* Can I borrow your net, Dylan?

DYLAN: Sure. *(SAMIRA drags the net across the pool and lifts it out.)* Catch anything?

SAMIRA: A starfish!

DYLAN: No hidden loot, then?

CARLOS wanders over to a rock on the other side of the cove.

CARLOS: Hey, I think I've found something! It's stuck between the rocks.

DYLAN and SAMIRA join him.

SAMIRA: It's just an old bottle! *(She turns to go back to her rock pool.)*

CARLOS: No, wait! *(holding it up to the light)* There's something in it! *(excitedly)* Maybe it's a treasure map!

DYLAN: *(taking the bottle from CARLOS)* It's a note.

SAMIRA: *(coming closer, more interested now)* A message in a bottle! Cool!

DYLAN: Go on, Carlos: you found it so
            you open it!

*DYLAN hands the bottle back to CARLOS.
CARLOS unscrews the lid of the bottle and
takes out the note.*

CARLOS: *(reading aloud) Dear Finder.*

DYLAN: The writing looks really old.
            Look at the date! That's during
            World War II!

SAMIRA: Shh, Dylan. Let him read it.
            What does it say, Carlos?

CARLOS: *(clears throat) Dear Finder, I send this message in a bottle and I hope it meets a friend across the sea. I hate that we are at war now. I wonder if there is a boy like me in the enemy's country who also wishes we could stop fighting? If you find this, I hope you will write back. Yours sincerely, Hans.* He has written his address – a street in Bremerhaven, Germany.

SAMIRA: Germany is so far away *(points out to sea)*. It must have taken ages to get here. That's amazing!

CARLOS: *(grumbling)* Yeah, but it's not a treasure map, is it?

DYLAN: *(thinking aloud)* It might be to someone. Granddad would love this. He could have been the kind of boy Hans was hoping to reach.

CARLOS: So let's show him.

They run back to DYLAN'S house.

DYLAN: Granddad, a letter for you!

GRANDDAD: What's this? It's all sandy.

DYLAN: We found it in a bottle in your cove.

GRANDDAD: Well, bless me. What lovely handwriting. *(reads then removes his glasses, eyes glistening with tears)*

DYLAN: *(quietly)* Should we not have brought it, Granddad?

GRANDDAD: That's very moving. Those were terrible times. *(gets up out of his chair)*

DYLAN: Where are you going?

GRANDDAD: To write back, of course. *(The children smile at each other, knowing they have taken the letter to exactly the right person.)* But I think I'll use a stamp rather than a bottle. I wouldn't want Hans and his relatives to wait another few decades to get an answer.

Lost for Words

By Julia Golding
Illustrated by Emi Ordas

Do you remember whatshisname
Who shared a doodah with thingy?
He lived near to that so-and-so
And had a whatsit, didn't he?

A whatsit? No! A thingamabob
For I saw it once with oojit,
Great gizmos on its you-know-what,
I'm surprised you could forget it.

Find out more ...

Find out what happens when Max looks after Rover for the weekend in *Finding Rover*.

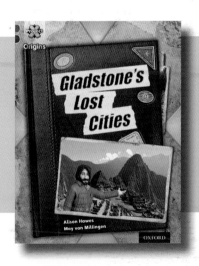

Join Gladstone Day on his exploration of famous lost cities in *Gladstone's Lost Cities*.